Other books by this author:

Amelia's Secrets

Ghosts of Amelia & Other Tales

by
Maggie Carter-de Vries

authorHOUSE®

AuthorHouse™
1663 Liberty Drive, Suite 200
Bloomington, IN 47403
www.authorhouse.com
Phone: 1-800-839-8640

First published by AuthorHouse 12/8/2008

ISBN: 978-1-4389-3818-9 (sc)

Printed in the United States of America
Bloomington, Indiana

This book is printed on acid-free paper.

ESIDENTS AND VISITORS ALIKE ARE charmed by the beauty and serene attractions of our little island of Amelia. The wide sandy beaches, white capped waves rolling and lapping upon the shores lure us to swim, surf, hunt shells and sharks teeth, build sand castles and lather on suntan lotion as we bronze away the lazy days of summer at the beach or stroll historic Centre Street, while licking feverishly at ice creams melting and dripping down our hands onto the sidewalks.

While least known among this tranquility drift the restless spirits of those who once walked on these streets, lived in these beautiful old homes in an era of refined gentility, and died too soon or in ways unnatural.

Whether you are a believer or not, it is my intention to pass these stories on to you as they were told to me, not as a historical exercise but as one does in passing on legends.

Therefore, sit back, relax and enjoy maybe you too will become a believer in the end.

Table of Contents

Acknowledgements

$\mathscr{I}$T GOES WITHOUT SAYING THIS book could not have been written had not the spirits of those who linger beyond the grave, refusing to pass on into eternal light because they so enjoy wandering among the living ignoring their ethereal existence, prodded me on.

I do wish to thank The Amelia Island Museum of History for their valuable assistance for again allowing me to peruse their library of history and archives. The sketch of Sara Alice Broadbent was found among those tombs and is credited to Mrs. Alice Youngblood's writings from an article of notes written by her in 1940 when she was lucky enough to spend several hours talking to the normally-reserved Sara Alice. Furthermore, the newspaper article about the Nassau Sound Affair and the information on the 215 S. 5th Street haunting were found at the museum.

I wish to credit Brandon Redding of Tampa, Florida for the photos containing the orbs on the book cover (Bosque Bello Cemetery) and Kate Bailey's tree.

I wish to express my gratitude to Nick Deonas and Mary Agnes Wolff-White for the stories they told me, and I pass on to you.

This book is dedicated to the residents and visitors of Amelia Island and especially to my grandson, Andrew Jace Miller.

An Angel of a Ghost

March 19, 1882

11/15/2008

$\mathcal{C}$ HARLES ANGEL WAS CALLED TO the home of his long time friend and former employee, sixty-five year old John Waas, "to discuss a matter of importance", by a personal visit on Saturday and by the two notes Waas sent to Angel & Friend's bakery the following day, Sunday being the day of the murder. Now Mr. Angel had an appointment to drive out to the beach with Mr. Koerner but upon receiving the last note and being a kind and gentle man decided instead to call on Mr. Waas at the requested 4:00 p.m. time instead, saying, "I believe I'll go and see what the old man wants. He has been rather despondent lately and may want a favor of me."

It is not known what conversation the two men had or in what manner Mr. Waas was received, but several witnesses passing by the residence moments prior the shooting heard calm talking, even laughter between the two gentlemen and one woman saw the two through the open parlor door, Angel standing on the piazza poised to leave and Waas sitting, obviously relaxed.

According to the Florida Mirror March 25, 1882 It is a theory, and circumstances warrant it, that Angel had said good-bye and turned to leave, when Waas hailed him, asking him to "hold on", he turned and without a moment's warning the deadly contents of the gun poured into his throat severing the jugular vein and parotid artery on the left side and lodging in the spine and base of the skull. Death ensued almost instantaneously and he had only time to breathe the accursed name of his slayer.

Mr. Waas, after committing the horrible deed, hastened to the back part of the house, swallowing a large dose of opium as he passed through an inner room and reaching the outhouse fastened the door on the inside, and with a razor, inflicted the wounds which consequently caused his death. On the left arm he succeeded in severing all the arteries, five in number but having to use the left hand after the gash was inflicted had not sufficient strength to cut very deep in the right arm and succeeded only in severing one small artery. He was removed to his room where he lingered until Monday night. He recovered consciousness and asked if his victim was dead yet expressing no penitence but on the contrary exalting in the deed. He refused all nourishment and attention saying he wanted to die and would die. He died at nine o'clock on Monday evening.

Immediately after the tragic occurrence there was found in the room a letter addressed to his daughter, on the envelope was written:

"To Louise"
Don't send for a doctor.
Don't disturb me.
Don't take off my clothes.

A package of bandages was also found to which a note was pinned the following,"Use these bandages to tie up my arms." The letter to his daughter was a long one, written with deliberation, and was principally of a private nature; containing direction to his daughter and the only allusion to the crime was the following sentence, which shows that the deed was contemplated before the shooting: "I know I have committed a horrible deed but I am not sorry for it." He also directed her where to find five letters which he had written and which were to be delivered to their respective addresses, which were, Mr. G. Stark, Mr. Frank Waas, Mr. Henry Muller, Mr. J. A. Ellerman and Mr. O. S. Oakes. The letters relate mostly to private affairs and throw no light on the subject.

Mr. Waas was for many years a citizen of this place enjoying the confidence of this place and respect of the entire community. He was regarded as an honest and industrious though eccentric German. He leaves behind a large family who are plunged in deepest grief in contemplating his horrid crimes. It is not known if he had other relatives living.

Further evidence Mr. Waas had been planning this brutal murder were his remarks to several friends that he would not live long, the recent making of his will and his wife's grave had also been repaired with the removal of a child's body to make room for his own.

Beautiful, much younger, Regina Waas was John's second wife from his home in Baden-Baden, Germany and they had been married but a short time.

There were whispers around town that Charles Angel had fathered John and Regina Waas' last child, the child that was removed from the cemetery plot, the child that caused Regina's early death. Whispers of a death bed confession by Regina to John of a terrible deed. Is this the reason John became crazed enough to kill his former employer and friend?

Charles Angel's restless spirit has been reported to roam near his grave site in St. Peter's Cemetery on the anniversary of his death, visit him there. Mayhap you will be the one to learn the truth if Charles is so willing to tell after all these years.

Or visit John M. Waas' resting place in Bosque Bello Cemetery where he appears to be resting in peace with both of his wives.

Williams House

Corner of 9th and Ash Streets

OUNDS OF GIRLISH LAUGHTER ON a warm July day awakened Will as he lay napping away the pleasant afternoon following a delicious lunch and a brief summer rain shower so typical of Amelia Island. He lay quietly listening, trying to think who it could possibly be? To his knowledge none of the guests staying at the Williams House Bed & Breakfast had a child with them. He rolled over, gave his pillow a good fluffing and tried to go back to sleep but the tinkling sound of laughter began again and after a few minutes curiosity got the best of him. Rising he peeked through the lace curtains puzzled to find an empty verandah. Walking over to the rocking chair beside the door he sat down to mull this over when an over whelming desire to go for a bike ride came over him. Now this isn't something Will did on a regular basis. Helpless to resist he found himself going to the garage, climbing on one of the bikes and heading downtown. In just a few minutes he found himself at the gate to St. Peter's Episcopal Church Cemetery, leaning the bike against the fence, pushing the squeaking gate open and wandering through the cemetery, a place he had never been before. His feet seemed to know the path to take him on this mysterious journey and when he came to a stop he found himself reading the tombstone dedicated to a young child; Sallie Williams, inscribed July 14, 1884, exactly 112 years ago to the date he was standing there! So young, what happened? Was she sad? No, she was laughing on the verandah, in high spirits, inviting him to come out, follow her to this place, spend time with her. She was obviously accustomed to having people around her as history tells of friends and family and many parties at the Williams House in its heyday.

From the first day Will's brother Chris and his partner Dick were shown the Williams house by their realtor they knew it was occupied by lingering spirits as she told them she "had a legal responsibility" to reveal the information to them. Upon entering the main hall of the old, empty, badly in need of restoration home Dick said he "had a feeling that someone had wrapped their arms around him in welcome."

Images of several spirits have appeared in a mirror on the main stair landing so often it had to be removed and at 3:30 a.m. one morning a gentleman dressed in grey, wearing a tall hat had appeared at the foot of Chris' bed.

Though there are a number of spirits roaming the Williams House, there is no cause for fear as this home has always been filled with laughter and love from the original family to the present owners.

Sara Alice

"Crane Island Woman"

ETWEEN THE GLOOMY DEPTHS OF the dark waterway and the main island of Fernandina Beach roams the solitary figure of a woman. Tall and gaunt, dressed in feed sacking, barefooted and carrying an old rifle, she plods along.

It is along the long stretch of Fletcher Avenue that the headlights of your car will discover her. She comes to town, wading across from her home on Crane Island, near the airport at low tide, to buy provisions.

Her name is Sara Alice and she will accept a ride if you offer, sitting quietly in the back seat. She will not partake of any conversation and indeed if you try to strike one up she will most often simply disappear. Many have experienced her doing just this.

Her father, John Wood Broadbent, purchased Crane Island (also called Coney Island) in 1882 from Mr. Noyes. It is there on this peaceful island that Sara Alice and her sister Ester Ann were raised.

Ester Ann was a dainty little thing full of life, laughter and fun. Sara Alice, on the other hand was a different sort of girl. She was said to be able to talk to the animals of the wooded island and spent hours roaming the forest in search of game and fish. Many a night she stayed out until daybreak, sleeping under the stars, staying away from people.

Ester Ann married and moved to Fernandina while Sara Alice stayed on to help her father, who was a black smith. She had no desire to marry and leave her beloved island.

After her father passed away she became more reclusive and strange. It is said she would shoot at anyone who dared set foot on her island. She armed herself with a variety of old guns, shooting at those who came to loot and steal.

The mystery unfolds in the wee hours of November 14, 1952 when a fire destroyed her home. No trace of Sara Alice was ever found.

Did she die in the fire? Folks say no, because the body was never found. Did she slip away into the night and hide in the dense forest? Perhaps, or perhaps not. She befriended the animals and possibly it was time for them to befriend her.

It was told she had come to town a few days prior to the fire to receive an inheritance from the bank, insisting on taking it in gold coins. This too was never found. Did she take this with her or did the arsonists kill her, dispose of the body and take her coins as well?

However, through the years many have told of picking up a tall, gaunt woman along Fletcher Avenue as she was plodding along toward town.

Is this Sara Alice? If so, why does she continue her journey? What is she seeking, provisions in town or revenge on those who destroyed her home?

Kate Bailey's Tree

Corner of South 7th & Ash Streets

HORSE DRAWN BUGGIES SLOWLY EVOLVED into larger, more modern automobiles and Kate McDonald Bailey watched the progress of it all from the windows and porches of her home.

If you had told her of the future events that would occur in her life over the ever increasing traffic in the city of Fernandina she would have laughed at the mere idea.

Kate and her husband, Effingham W. Bailey began construction of their home in 1892, the project was completed in 1895 and they moved into their magnificent home. Effingham, an agent for a regional steamship company, selected mail order plans from noted architect George W. Barber of Knoxville, Tennessee. He and Kate were given their lot by her parents, who lived next door. They utilized local shipbuilders and carpenters to build it for them.

Life was idyllic in the Queen Anne style home until the fateful day Kate learned the city was planning to cut down the wonderful old oak tree that had stood for over a hundred years on Ash Street (on the South side of her home.) Kate could not stand the thought of looking out her windows or sitting in her porch swing and not seeing the stately tree. She asked Effingham to see into the matter but upon returning home he informed Kate that there was no stopping the destruction of the tree.

The more she thought about it, the more determined Kate was to save the tree. But, how was she a solitary sole and a woman, to go about doing so?

On the fateful day the crew showed up with their saws and axes they found Kate sitting under the tree with a shotgun in hand daring anyone to take the first strike! The men, astonished at her courage and audacity, reported back to the city fathers who came out to see what was going on. They implored Kate to remove herself so the men could get on with their work. But of course she would not. She sat there well into the night, guarding her tree.

The city fathers relented and built the street around the tree where it stands to this day.

Folks claim they have seen Kate on clear moonlight nights sitting quietly, holding her shotgun, guarding her tree. Photographing the tree just after dusk others have captured tiny orbs floating in the tree and also a ghostly face can be seen among the branches.

Prescott House

120 North 6th Street

 HIS MAGNIFICENT HOME WAS BUILT in 1876 by Josiah Prescott, owner of J. H. Prescott's Mercantile Store, the building presently known as the Palace saloon. It is of the Victorian style with Chippendale railings and intricate woodwork, located in the most desirable "Silk Stocking District" of Fernandina Beach.

I, the writer of this story had the enormous pleasure of owning this home in the early 1990's and experienced the nocturnal visits by the apparition of a young girl who delighted in rocking in a particular chair and stopping the mantle clocks and my grandfather clock.

I first saw her standing in the doorway between the kitchen and small office (which originally was a porch). I was working late one night at the kitchen table on paper work for my restaurant. Both children were upstairs asleep. A movement out of the corner of my eye made me look up to see her standing there, wearing a white night gown, her dark hair brushing her shoulders. The kitchen wing was added onto the house around 1920 and I believe she did not cross over the threshold because it did not exist in her time.

I initially thought it was my daughter, Tania, whose bedroom was located above the kitchen. Thinking that she might possibly be sick I spoke to her but she disappeared. Puzzled I arose and went up the servants stairs only to find Tania sound asleep dressed in her favorite sleep garb of boxers and sloppy T-shirt. Immediately I knew there was a presence other than myself and my two children in the house. The next morning I found an old, small silver ring with a black onyx setting near the kitchen entrance. Neither I nor the children had ever seen the ring before. I still have it in my jewelry box and take it out every now and then to wonder and ponder over.

One night after returning home from a movie we found a rocking chair in the den rocking to and fro on its own accord.

We owned the house for almost seven years and during that time I saw the girl numerous times. There was not a pattern nor did there seem to be any particular reason for her appearances. I do know that she was not happy about our selling the house. We remained there for six months after the sale and during that time I never saw her again.

The reason I know she was sad to see us go is because the grandfather clock and mantle clocks would stop…no matter how many times I started them they always stopped again and again. After moving into another Victorian House a few blocks away the same clocks ran continuously, never stopping even once.

The Guv'nor's Manse

Corner of Alachua & North 5th Street

CROSS THE STREET FROM FIRST Baptist Church sits a home with quite a history. Dr. Percy N. Richardson, an African-American druggist and physician whose drugstore was located at 18 N. 4th Street built it in 1902.

In 1904 he sold the house to Samuel A. Swann, who sold it to Jesse C. Hise. Court house records of November 1905 show that Hise sold it to Annie E. Johns, wife of Everett E. Johns. After being defeated for re-election as sheriff of Starke, Florida, Johns was offered a position with the Fernandina Sheriff's office by his friend, Sheriff Higginbotham.

Everett, Annie and their infant son, Charley, had lived there for just a few months when Everett was summoned to the beach early one morning to investigate the theft of some fishing nets. Annie became concerned when he had not returned for the mid-day meal and doubly concerned when by nightfall she had not heard from him. Higginbotham led a search party that found Everett's horse pulling an empty buggy along the old shell beach road. Later that night, his body was found lying on the beach.

Opinion has it he was murdered to prevent him from testifying in an upcoming Federal case, in which he was the key witness. His wife and son remained in the house until the widow sold it to Noble A. Hardee on February 16, 1910. They then returned to Starke where Charley grew up and became a member of the House of Representatives in 1935. Later he was elected to the Senate, serving as President of the Senate at the time Governor Daniel McCarty died. As President of the Senate, it fell to Charley to finish out McCarty's term as governor from 1953 to 1955.

During the passing years, the figure of a man, dressed in old-style garb with a badge on his coat has been seen walking along the beach near Slider's Seaside Grill, where the old shell road once ended. These sightings only occur during hurricane force storms in the month of November.

"Felippa"

Voodoo Priestess/Old Town 1817

$\mathcal{T}$HE MERE MENTION, WHISPERED IN the ears of naughty children, was enough to cause the very breath and heartbeats to cease and the source of naughtiness to desist in an instant. Rare daylight sightings of the turban wrapped crone with skin of polished, weathered mahogany, head held erect as befitted a voodoo priestess, as she walked the streets of Fernandina on the Isle of Amelia, scattered young and old alike into their dwellings to hide until even her shadow passed. She was known to make the dead awaken, the loveless to be loved, cure the ill and barren to conceive. On the other hand, for the passing of gold across her palm all kinds of terrible curses could be conjured against those to who was born ill will.

With this in mind, on a dark moonless night, dressed in black and clutching gold coins tied in a handkerchief, Demity slipped quietly from her house to Felippa's hut on the edge of a creek bank. Every night sound caused her to stop and tremble at what she was about. Her desire for another's man had driven her in desperation to this final act. Stepping hesitatingly upon the low stoop she raised her hand to knock just as the door swung open and Felippa bade her enter, "I have been expecting you," she said pointing to a low stool before the fire. The heart you desire belongs to another, it takes powerful magic to break the spell of this love and the consequences cannot always be sure."

"But will he be mine; will he love me and only me? She demands" Anxious now that she was there to get the deed over without a care for the dire warnings. Jerking her hand away from Felippa's touch as she passed the gold coins, causing them spill across the dirt floor but not quick enough to prevent Felippa from seeing a vision of the selfish, mean spirited woman before her. Demity cursed Felippa for her clumsiness. "Hurry, mix your potion, cast your spell you stupid old crow, I must be gone from this vile place!"

Felippa knelt before the fire adding numerous ingredients into a large black pot, chanting as she went. At long last she poured the elixir into a cup instructing Demity to drink as she placed ashes from the fireplace on her forehead and a necklace with an amulet of the elixir around her neck with instructions to place the liquid in her hearts desires' drink at first opportunity, but before rise of the next full moon, a fortnight away.

Not waiting to hear more, Demity ran out into the night the vile taste of the elixir rising like bile in her throat. Clutching the amulet around her throat she hastened home shaking as she slipped quietly through the door.

Almost a fortnight later her sister lies in bed ill with the ague. Demity must act as hostess to her brother-in-laws' card guests and opportunity finally presents itself to complete the spell. Entering the parlor with whiskey for his guests; Autry, Irwin and Hubbard she is surprised to see more tables set up and guests than expected. Nervously passing drinks around as to not mix them up she hurries back to the butler's pantry for more glasses. Upon returning she finds her brother-in-law, being the ever proper host, has given his drink to an ugly toad of a man with yellowing teeth, mottled skin and stains on his waistcoat. Turning toward her as she enters the room his eyes light up with love and adoration.

Upstairs Felippa chants a singsong litany, a sly smile on her face, as she places another poultice on Demity's sister's chest.

*Note: Felippa was indeed real and lived in Old Town, the original settlement of Fernandina. Lots are noted in public records on Ladies Street as being deeded to her in 1811 and 1821.

She is mentioned in a novel written by Frank Slaughter, "The Golden Isle" 1947.

Also her descendant named Felippa is mentioned in my novel, "Amelia's Secret's" 2008.

Fort Clinch Hauntings

$\mathcal{L}$OCATED AT THE ENTRANCE TO the St. Mary's River and the Cumberland Sound the site was occupied by various military troops since 1736. Construction of a fort, later named Fort Clinch in honor of General Duncan L. Clinch, began in 1847. A pentagonal brick fort with both inner and outer walls, Fort Clinch was a safe haven for blockade runners during the Civil War. Briefly occupied by Confederate forces, its recapture by Federal troops in early 1862 gave the Union control of the adjacent Georgia and Florida coasts.

On the first weekend of each month re-enactors take over the fort turning it into a place of living history. Men in Union blue strut boldly about carrying their weapons, officers shouting orders, while their counterparts in Confederate Gray cower in the dungeons. Women dressed in period clothing cook meals over open fires while children play games of a day gone by. After the candle light service and visitors have gone to their homes, and campers to their tents, the winds blow gently across the parade ground ushering in the softly moaning sighs of the night.

Guards huddle closely around the campfires, eyes peering into the dark night as the stories of the restless ones begin. First there is the Civil War nurse who takes her duties seriously, wearing her white cap, basket of neatly folded bandages on her arm. She is often seen in the sally port, or tunnel entrance, which leads to the parade ground she wanders tirelessly seeking wounded to treat.

A park ranger, back in 1952 walking through the parade grounds on a balmy July night was taken by surprise when he encountered the figures of four Union soldiers. They marched as far as the flag pole then simply disappeared into thin air. The really odd thing was that none of them had heads! At first he was hesitant to report this strange occurrence, but only a few nights later again encountered the soldiers. This time there were only three of them. Gathering his courage he bravely ventured to ask where the fourth man was and was duly surprised when informed that. "He did not feel well enough to march that night." Realizing the apparitions were not imaginary he immediately reported them to his superior officer who informed him they were only a few of the many reported stories throughout the years.

Merrick-Simmons House

102 S. 10th Street

$\mathcal{T}$HE EARLIEST RECORDED OCCUPANT OF this pre-civil war home was Chloe Merrick, a New York teacher who came to Fernandina in 1863 under the auspices of the National Freedman's Relief Association of New York who owned the house as the agent for the National Freedman's Relief Association from June 1863 until 1865. During this time she met Harrison Reed, the newly appointed Direct Tax Commissioner of Florida, who was so impressed with her work that he used his political position to purchase General Finnegan's abandoned home (where the school board occupies the old high school on Atlantic Avenue) in a tax sale to serve as an orphanage for homeless freedman children on Amelia Island. Chloe Merrick left to teach in North Carolina upon the closing of the orphanage in 1865. As Florida's new Governor, in 1869 Reed traveled to North Carolina, proposed and they were married at Merrick's home in Syracuse, New York on August 10, 1869. To this union was born one son, Harrison Merrick Reed.

There have been several owners of the property since Chloe, with the longest being John Simmons (1899-1925) owner of the Ice House located at the rear of the property and partner along with Effingham Bailey (Bailey House) and Louis Hirth (Palace Saloon) of the Fernandina Trolley Lines. He reportedly made the trolley run from Centre Street to the Simmons House so he would not have to walk downtown or to Main Beach.

The old icehouse located at the rear of the property is reported to have been the site of activities of unspeakable disciplinary activities performed by the Klu Klux Klan to whip those persons into line who wandered off the path of proper behavior whether they were black or white. There often have been unexplainable sounds from behind the house.

There is reportedly more than one ghost occupying Merrick-Simmons House. A couple renting the house in 1995 had feelings of not being welcomed. Found in the dusty attic was a lone piece of furniture. Positioned exactly in the center was a small rocking chair surrounded by a circle, perfectly free of dust. Naturally curious they left the chair where it was. It was not long before they were astonished to see the spirit of a little girl going up the stairs to rock in the chair late at night. After the chair was moved to the downstairs parlor it was seen to rock gently to and fro as with a will of its own.

Jim, a pastry chef at "Horizons Restaurant" rented the upstairs, third floor for a short period of time told me he definitely was not welcome! He returned late one afternoon to find two of the three upstairs windows completely covered in blue flies. Strangely the center window did not have a single fly on it! Trying to shoo the flies away was to no avail, they immediately returned to the two windows. Haddock Pest Control was called to fumigate and after performing the service returned a short time later and could find not a trace of the flies, dead or alive! It was as if the incident never happened!

Standing in the attic with the present owner, Monty Stewart, (1998-today) much to my amazement, he affirmed he has always had problems with flies at that particular window.

I had a wonderful feeling of euphoria and love while exploring this wonderful old home with Monty and his brother George. I honestly feel that the spirits that abound here, especially the little girl belong to the original owners who built the house and those records remain unknown at this time.

Eppe's House

Ash & 10th & Street

*I*N 1880 THOMAS JEFFERSON EPPES, great-great grand Son of President Thomas Jefferson came to Fernandina employed as a baggage master for the railroad by way of Monticello, Florida.

Dashing, handsome and well connected none of the towns daughters paraded before this eligible bachelor could persuade him to tie the knot and all were set to not like his young bride, Katie Shaylor from Archer, Florida who took the town by storm in September 1883, for no other reason than "she is not our kind" and beautiful to boot.

Possessed of a willful spirit, long black tresses flowing to her waist, dark eyes flashed and sparkled with life, enchanting to men of all ages our Katie loved to dance the night away at every opportunity but Jeff's job kept him away more often than a newly-wed bride should be left alone.

Not one to stand on social etiquette Katie went about as she pleased, without a chaperone, driving her buggy about town and to the masquerade balls causing tongues to wag.

In February of 1884 upon returning from a lengthy business trip Jeff's' brother-in-law, George Dewson met him at the station visibly upset by a sworn secret his wife Mary who was Katie's sister had told her. A secret he could not retain and one that set in motion an act that would tear not only the two men's families asunder but the whole town as well.

Katie confided to Mary in tears claiming that Ferdinand Suhrer, manager of the Mansion House Hotel where they were living while their home was being built, had come to her room and laid his hand on her breast and had tried to assault her.

Furious as any husband would be, Jeff immediately went about town seeking a pistol and a whip; hastened to the Mansion House Hotel and called his henceforth friend Ferdinand outside to the steps where he recited the charges against him and began whipping him. Grabbing hold of the whip, Ferdinand denied the charges. Where upon Jeff reached into his coat pocket, drew out a pistol and shot Ferdinand in the upper, left chest. Major Suhrer, looking astonished, fell to the porch, asking, "why,

why, why?" "I may be a dead man, Jeff, but as God is my witness, I did not…" Ferdinand died about five hours later leaving a grieving widow and six children to fend for themselves.

Jeff and George Dewson turned themselves in to the sheriff to await trial which followed in May in Jacksonville due to a change of venue. It took longer to select a jury than it did for the jury to return with a sentence of not guilty to the amazement of the over crowded court room.

Katie and Jeff were blessed with the birth of their first son, Thomas Jefferson Eppes, Jr. on September 4th and another son Douglas in December of 1885 who died, followed soon thereafter by Katie's death in June 1886.

On her death bed, she made this confession to Jeff, "I lied."

This was done to make Jeff jealous so he would stop leaving her alone for days on end. The ghost of a woman with long dark hair, streaked with white, has often been seen at the house on the corner of Ash & 10th Streets. She appeared to relatives who lived there many years ago telling them the streak of white "is my mark of Cain for telling a lie that caused the death of an innocent man".

- The complete story can be read in my novel "Amelia's Secrets" released July 2008.

Mrs. Nettie Thompson

23 South 7th Street

PROBABLY THE LIVELIEST AND MOST well known ghost is Mrs. Nettie Thompson who refuses to give up her pretty little Victorian residence on Seventh Street, roaming the halls at night her black taffeta dress rustling as she disappears through a wall where a door once led to the kitchen; traipsing up and down stairs her wooden sole shoes making enough noise to wake the dead.

She has a fetish for keeping things in an orderly fashion and tends to move jewelry, hairbrushes and small items from the right side of the dresser to the left, leaving the scent of candles wafting behind her as she goes about her chores.

Former owner, Sheila Fountain, says babysitters refused to sit for her after having seen Mrs. Thompson rocking in a chair while Mrs. Fountain's children were sleeping in another room.

Mrs. Galloni, after purchasing it, was at first afraid to enter the home until she decided it was amusing that all Mrs. Thompson wanted was to have the jewelry on the left side of the dresser and as long as she complied all was well.

Mrs. Thompson died unexpectedly in Miami from gas inhalation and the story goes that she has returned to guard a hidden treasure, or maybe she just lingers because she loves the home her husband, Pratt Thompson built for her many years ago.

Weimer House

604 Ash Street

*T*HIS HOUSE DATES BACK BEFORE the Civil War and during the war the third floor attic was reported to have been used as a hospital for injured soldiers by the Union Army.

During the time span it was a home and restaurant (The Christmas House/Rudolpho's) 1995-2006 MaryAnn, Grace and Andy lived upstairs and ran the restaurant downstairs as well as sharing the home with more than one apparition.

One evening a guest seated near the front asked MaryAnn who the little girl was, with pointing at a table close to the kitchen doors, as the child had been there for some time by herself. When they both turned to look at the child was no longer there but the description matched the same one given by more than one guest who had seen her previously. Her attire is always exactly the same, never changing and appeared to be late 1800's.

Another ghostly visitor is a gentleman dressed in the same period of clothing, with a tall hat and cane that walks through the left front parlor and straight into the back room late at night, quite unnerving.

This home was owned by the Weimer family in the late 1890's whose daughter, Wilhemenia married Frank "Francis" Joseph Suhrer, and son of Ferdinand Suhrer who was murdered by T. J. Eppes in 1884 and to this union was born three sons and two daughters. One of those sons was Ferdinand Charles Suhrer, born Oct. 29, 1919 and as of this writing he resides in Pacifica, California.

His son, Andrew S. Suhrer is the author of "The Flying Dutchmen", written in 2008 depicting the life of Ferdinand through his Civil War battles.

Strange Happenings at
215 South 5th Street

HE HOUSE WAS PURCHASED THE first week of January, 2000, by Robert and Brenda Jackson, of Atlanta, Georgia.

January 7-The Jacksons arrived late, with Mrs. Jackson's mother, who may be interested in living in the house. When Mrs. Harris was in the master bathroom, the heavy wooden doorsill fell near her feet. Later, another very loud crash was heard in the next bedroom by the Jacksons. They thought Mrs. Harris had fallen down, and went to check on her. Mrs. Harris was in the adjacent bedroom reading, and had not heard a noise at all. An odor of decay prevented the family from sleeping well. Mrs. Harris was extremely cold and could not seem to ever get warm all night. The odor could not be detected the next day.

January 8-The Jacksons were joined by family members who live in Fernandina Beach. As the party was going out the door to dinner, Mr. Jackson was alone in the kitchen for a moment. He heard a loud "sniff" beside him and looked to see if his wife was on the other side of the refrigerator. No one was there. After returning from dinner, Mr. Jackson and his brother-in-law were talking in the kitchen. Movement caught his eye and the heavy, iron chandelier was swinging gently above their heads. Other guests entered the kitchen and observed the swinging. Finally, a guest reached up to the 8 ft. fixture and stopped it. Try as they may, no one could get the fixture to swing by jumping up and down and running through the house, etc.

January 15-The bedroom floors were being refinished, so the Jacksons were sleeping on an air mattress in the breakfast room, adjacent to the kitchen. Sometime in the early morning hours, they were awakened by a vibrate/beeping/vibrate sequence of noises. The vibrating noise sounded like a pager, then three beeps, then the vibrating sound again, sounding as if in the room. Upon awakening, Mrs. Jackson told her husband that his pager was beeping. He got up to check his pager in the hallway and discovered it had not beeped; neither does it make the same sound. They never figured out what the sound was.

January 21-A family friend and handyman was painting at the house. He had not been told anything about the strange happenings. As he slept on the air mattress that night, he had a very disturbing dream that a woman in a white dress was coming down the hallway, calling out several names. She seemed to be trying to communicate with him, but did not seem to be menacing. Nevertheless, he was frightened enough to leave the house at 4:00 AM and drive back to Atlanta.

January 22-The Jacksons arrived and were sleeping on the air mattress. Sometime in the early morning, they heard a noise from the mattress itself, a slight sliding of the mattress on the bare floor. They both assumed the other had shifted it by moving. About ten minutes later, both heard the noise again, and Mr. Jackson jumped up. He had felt something pushing up from beneath the air mattress. He did not go back to bed, and arose for the day. Coincidentally, Mrs. Jackson remembered having what she described as one of the best dreams of her life, in which she encountered several people for whom she felt deep love, and they loved her! One of them, a woman was having a problem with her eyes, and when Mrs. Jackson touched her, she felt such strong feelings that Mrs. Jackson cried in her dream. These people were not familiar to her, but she awakened with a feeling of love and happiness.

*   This article was found in the files at The Amelia Museum of History and is courtesy of the museum.

*   The author is unknown but more than likely was Mr. or Mrs. Jackson.

The Book Loft

214 Centre Street

*T*HE SMELL OF BOOKS OLD and new greets eager readers as they pass into this place of knowledge and adventure with the mere turning of a page.

Row upon rows of bookcases lines the walls and down the hall of the first floor and more of the same beckon up the winding stairs above.

Little do most folk know that on many a morning as the key is turned in the lock it is with trepidation and anticipation; hearts pound wondering if the lady ghost who takes down the books from the top shelves upstairs has been busy the night before stacking books neatly as she empties the cases one by one making their new day a busy one indeed.

Employees tell without hesitation and with assurance, they have seen her leaning over the top floor balustrade observing them at work when they know for sure they are the only ones in the book store.

Palace Saloon

Centre & Second Street
Uncle Charlie Beresfords Ghost

THE PALACE SALOON WAS BUILT in 1878 by Josiah Prescott as a dry goods store until it changed hands in 1903 and has been Florida's longest operating bar since then, with one exception during Prohibition when the Palace was the last saloon to stop serving booze and for a time it was an ice cream parlor.

Uncle Charlie also held a record of being the employee to have worked there for the longest time, 1906-1960 when he died in a back room one night after his bartending shift.

Legends surrounding Charlie are many; one is the bartender's habit of tossing a coin to see if it would balance on the cleavage of the breasts of the carved female figures of the bar. Any coin that falls behind the bar belongs to Uncle Charlie and woe to the person who tries to retrieve it.

The door to Uncle Charlie's room in back opens and closes by itself, trash cans rattle up and down and glasses break as he goes about his nightly task of closing down the bar.

Customers and employees have been startled to hear the unplugged player piano begin to play on its own on more than one occasion. Lights go up and down, water starts running and bar stools topple over when no one is near.

I, for one, believe Uncle Charlie loved his job and home at The Palace Saloon and was a bit of a prankster who is determined to stick around for the amusement of us all.

St. Peter's Episcopal Church

Atlantic & 8th Streets
"The Cracked Mirror"

11/17/2008

*I*T IS THE CHRISTMAS SEASON and St. Peter's church and staff are busily decorating and preparing for next Sunday's special sermon and choral presentation. A parcel arrives and the young priest, thinking it to be a Christmas present, places it under the tree.

On Christmas Eve a letter arrives from Mrs. Duryee's daughter in New York, saying her mother has died and been cremated and a parcel containing her ashes had been sent to Amelia Island. The letter went on to give burial instructions for her mother's memorial and internment beside her father who had passed away some years before. Distressed because it is now Christmas Eve, a time of rejoicing, the priest decides to place the now known ashes of Mrs. Duryee on the bottom of the pier mirror Mr. Duryee had donated to the church many years ago until after Christmas.

This floor to ceiling mirror located in the vestry was donated by Major Duryee, so he could check his appearance before stepping out to sing in the choir each Sunday. Now it is a well know fact around town that the Duryee's were reputed to quarrel often and in public.

The priest was astonished when walking by the mirror the next morning to discover a large crack in the mirror running from the top down to the bottom where the box with Mrs. Duryee's ashes lay on the shelf. A parishioner, Miss Sophie Hawkins laughed saying, "Well, that's Mr. Duryee, all right. He didn't want her ashes sitting in front of his mirror."

211 S. 7th Street

HEN TANNER WARWICK WAS A toddler and just learning to talk his parents; Joe and Diane rented this lovely old home from Monty Stewart. On the day they signed the lease Diane jokingly asked Monty if the house had any ghosts and demanded he "give it up, you know you have to reveal it to us" she laughingly told him, "It's the law."

Monty was surprised at the question and reassured her he had never heard of any "happenings" concerned with the house.

On moving day Diane heard Tanner talking to someone in the library and curious as to whom it might be she ventured near only to find Tanner standing rigidly in the doorway repeating over and over, "No, I won't go with you", "No, I won't go with you!"

Peering into the empty room as she stooped down near him touching his shoulder, "Tanner, baby who are you talking to?" she asked.

"I don't want to go upstairs with the man in the black shirt," he said pointing toward the empty, far corner.

Shocked she looked again to make sure; there was no one there and hugging Tanner drew him into her arms and away from the room, soothing his fears saying, "Of course you don't have to go."

The Warwick's moved after a while and Monty Stewart now lives in this house. He hears doors opening and closing regularly and the library defiantly has a presence he tells me, but he has learnt to live with who or whatever insists on sharing his home. Alternatively, is he the intruder?

The Captains House

Old Town

11/11/2008

THE YELLOW FEVER EPIDEMIC STRUCK so cruelly and took the young son away from the mother's breast while her husband was away at sea. Night after night she stands in the tower window keeping watch for the ship that will bring him home to the sad loss of his boy.

She regrets her strict discipline that caused the last spanking, she gave and the refusal of a kiss to dry his tears. Instead she put him to bed with words of chastisement; words she now regrets.

This is the most accepted story of the woman in the tower window.

On the night of the first full moon after Mrs. Helen Litrico moved into the home she was startled by numerous people standing and parked outside her home, staring up at the tower window in search of a ghost. During the time she lived there she never saw anything and only reported hearing sounds of what she liked to believe were of an old house as it creaks and settles.

This home was used in the Pippi Longstocking film produced in 1988, staring Tami Erin and Eileen Brennan.

The Money Tree

Egan's Creek Treasure

$\mathcal{P}$IRATES TREASURE; A CHEST LADEN with gold, jewels and coins! The tale has been told for generations of bounty buried beneath a large oak tree with an anchor chain hanging from a limb pointing downwards the place to dig. It seems a pirate, mayhap it was Teach, had two of his men row him onto shore in order to bury his treasure, killing them with a chain, and burying them with the treasure marking it with the chain thrown over a limb of the tree.

Two brothers happened upon this tree, left to get a shovel but much to their dismay could not find the location again.

In the 1930's a Fernandina resident, Mr. George R. and two friends were hog hunting in the area of Ft. Clinch and happened upon this very same tree, and after spending the better part of the day digging, they unearthed a silver chest but were unable to extract it. Remembering the legend and its warning that if you left you could never find it again, the friends hurried away to seek help leaving George to guard the treasure.

Upon returning to the woods they were unable to relocate George, the tree or the treasure. Two days later George was discovered lying brutally beaten and exhausted on the beach claiming he had been chased by "a swirling mass of electricity through the woods until I fainted." His clothes were torn, his back was covered by bloody scratches and the sand around him soaked with blood. George lapsed into a coma lasting four days and bore the scars to the day he died.

Harrison Plantation
A1A

*T*HE GHOST OF A LADY dressed in black, wringing her lace gloved hands appears weeping at the top of the stairs at the midnight hour of the old Harrison Plantation home has circulated for years and intrigued ghost hunter Nick Deonas to the extent that he gained permission from the owners to spend the night in order to investigate and also to search the property for a treasure supposedly buried there during the Civil War.

After spending several fruitless nights, much to his disappointment, he could neither catch a glimpse of the lady nor did he find the much talked about treasure.

A Harrison descendant, Mrs. Catherine Prevatt of Cresent City, Florida wrote this explanation to the archaeologist studying the Dorion Dig area of the Plantation in 1971:

"Our grandmother, Isabel McQueen English Harrison, is the legendary ghost of Harrison Homestead-frequently seen by even tenants, many of whom have refused to live with "the lady with the lace mittens and bonnet, weeping on the stairway." She reportedly weeps because a son, Robert, sued for the Homestead following his father's death.

She also passed on the story of the slaughter of the Mission children that occurred late in the afternoon just prior to dinner and the eerie sounds that can still be heard of dying children and the clatter of dishes even today.

The house no longer stands, but to this day folk visiting the cemetery have a strange feeling of unrest. You must obtain the cemetery gate key from the Amelia Island Museum of History.

In addition to Harrison family members, a re-burial of Indian remains found on the Dorion Dig are interred in one corner of the cemetery in a mass grave.

*   Note: The Harrisons were related to President Harrison.

Florida House Inn

20-22 Third Street South

Florida's oldest operating hotel, having been built by David Yulee in 1857 prior to the Civil War, has a treasure trove of mysterious happenings, hauntings and things that go bump in the night.

The main dining room was used as a meeting place for the townspeople until a town hall could be built so it is not unusual for the sounds of furniture being moved about to be heard late on Tuesday nights.

Guests staying at the hotel have reported to be awakened by the figures of a man and small boy standing silently beside their bed. They had drowned while on a fishing trip and return searching the child's mother.

Another room has a lady ghost who moves apparel around during the night while yet another mischievously scatters things on the floor.

A small boy has been seen walking through the main dining room during the daytime when no one should be there and Mrs. Annie Leddy, owner from 1870 until the early 1900's, whispers instructions to the office workers while the smell of lavender permeates the air.

While counseling an errant employee a three-hole punch flew from the shelf from behind owner Diane Warwick's head and landed at her feet. Needless to say, it frightened her so much she jumped up and left. Later on Diane found out this employee delved deeply into witch craft and Ouija board reading.

"It seems they just want to let us know they are here, they normally aren't vindictive or malicious and the pranks are just that, pranks." Except for one instance when only staff was in the inn and suddenly the quiet was broken by a terrible racket coming from the men's restroom. "We all went running to see what had happened," Diane said and upon opening the door discovered the toilet bowl cover had been torn off and was lying broken on the floor."

Other dining room employees have been observed by a lady garbed in Victorian style as they go about their duties. No doubt this is Annie Leddy making sure things are done to her expectations.

Ghost hunters sought permission to come to the Florida House with their meters and cameras and while accompanied by Diane could discern the outline of a man of a rather tall stature in front of the cook stove and also of a woman in the hallway of the 1882 addition.

More Harrison Plantation

The Empty Whiskey Bottle and Swamp Ghosts

MAMIE AND MINNIE SHEPARD SPENT their early years in a little house on Harrison Plantation along with their mother, grandmother, aunts and uncles who worked on the plantation.

Their memories were a mixture of the pleasant, carefree days of all children and of the scary stories their mother told them of the swamp ghost meant to keep them close to home. This of course only added fuel to their curiosity and on a particularly boring summer afternoon; they decided to venture in that direction ....Sure enough something came lunging out of the dark regions, sending them tearing back home shaking and trembling in fear not daring to say a word to their mother of their disobedience.

When their stepfather came courting their mama, he would take the shortcut alongside the cemetery which lay between where he lived in American Beach and the Homestead. One Saturday night he had a pint of whisky in his back pocket as he headed her way, nearing the cemetery an odd feeling came over him making his feet move even faster, matching the rapid beat of his heart. Upon arriving at the Homestead, he removed the whisky flask from his pocket and sat down on the bottom step of the little house to take a swig in order to calm his nerves when to his surprise, he found the bottle to be totally empty, the top still on!

Their grandmother also told them a strange story about the cemetery...A long time ago she had to get up before daybreak to go to shuck oysters. In order to catch her ride, she had to pass by the cemetery to reach the road. One dark, fall morning as she walked by the cemetery smoking her pipe, she saw something that caused her to throw down her pipe and run screaming down the path to the waiting ride. After that two people had to walk up to the house and walk her down the path every morning and even this was done with much unease, and only because she needed the work.

Hanging of a Pirates Son
Old City Jail-3rd Street South

11/13/2008

HEN LOUIS AURY LEFT AMELIA Island, he not only left behind the memories of his infamous rule over the island but also an illegitimate son, Luc Simone Aury, who upon barely entering manhood was a renowned rapist, murderer and thief of the worst possible sort. Upon his capture he was sentenced to hang from the branch of a huge oak tree behind the City Jail.

However, the night before the hanging Aury, wishing to deprive the city of his humiliation, slit his own throat. In order to keep him alive just long enough to get him through the hanging, a surgeon was summoned to stitch and bandage his wound.

The next morning a large crowd had gathered to witness the execution of this famous criminal. They worked themselves into frenzy, screaming and shouting as he was dragged and prodded toward the tree, his wounded throat hidden by his buttoned up collar. Slowly, he climbed the gallows stairs, his arms pinned behind his back, eyes glaring menacingly at his captors while the noose was tightened ever so snugly round his neck.

Suddenly, the trap door sprung open, the stitches gave way and blood spewed over the horrified audience as his head is nearly decapitated. Women faint and children run screaming in terror from the horrible sight of the nearly headless man swinging to and fro.

Occasional moaning and sightings of Aury are reported coming from the site of the gallows behind the old jail which now houses The Amelia Island Museum of History.

Fire at St. Mary's Priory

Death of Sally Mays Call

ARAH WAS BORN JULY 6, 1854 to George W. and Sarah Starke Call, and was sent to Fernandina to attend St. Mary's Priory in 1870 by her Aunt Annie and Uncle Archibald Cole. Her mother had passed away in 1858 having not recovered from the birth of baby brother Rydon and her father Major Call's untimely death on the battle field at Fair Oakes during the Civil War left the children as wards of the Coles.

Located high on a hill surrounded by orange groves, in General Joseph Finnegan's beautiful colonial mansion which was purchased after the Civil War by Bishop Young of the Episcopal Diocese, this school for girls offered the best education of its time and has never been surpassed.

Sarah's curriculum included French, Italian, Drawing, Piano, Mathematics, Ordinary English, Natural Sciences and Development and Formation of the Voice and German.

Her favorite pastime was the game of tennis played on the smooth grass courts of old town, and she was often seen about town in her "uniform" of white swinging her racket, her pretty red ribbons holding back her raven hair.

She was an excellent student and one of the few allowed to remain up past curfew to study, reading by the light of a lone kerosene lamp. On the fateful night of February 16, 1871 as she reached up to turn down the lamp to extinguish it, she inadvertently turned the knob up instead causing flames to shoot upward and in her tired state she grabbed a book to cover the lamp thinking to smother the flames. The explosion was almost instantaneous as the book caused intense heat to build inside the lamp. Sally's nightgown and robe were on fire as were the curtains behind the desk and her horrible screams could be heard by the now totally awakened school.

The sight of Sally standing there, a human torch sent the girls scattering, out into the night. Someone grabbed blankets, threw Sally down, rolled her in them and carried her outside to safety. However, it was too late. Sarah Mays Call was dead at the age of sixteen.

After Sally's death the school was closed and moved to Jacksonville.

Joseph Finnegan's home no longer exists, in its place is the old Fernandina Beach High School which now serves as the School Board on Atlantic Avenue, and if you follow a path behind the building you will find a very pretty butterfly garden. In this garden it has been reported in the late midnight hours the figure of a girl dressed in old style tennis garb, carrying a tennis racket with long dark hair pulled back with red ribbons.

Hurricane of 1898

Strathmore Hotel's Dancing Beach Lady

HE STRATHMORE HOTEL WAS DESIGNED by Robert Schyler and built by the railroad in 1882. It was the center of beach activities and a favorite place for honeymooners as well as all tourists.

The tourist season of 1898 was winding down socially but there were still a few diehards staying at the Strathmore enjoying the warmth of Florida's balmy days, dreading the return to the dreary northern climates.

Among those was a newlywed couple from New York who had been spending their last week dancing the nights away in town at the Egmont Hotel while enjoying the sunny days at the beach.

The wife especially enjoyed rising early each morning for long, invigorating walks along the shore, or dancing among the waves in her bathing costume as she watched the sun rise in all its glory.

It was with much dismay to her new husband when he begged her to evacuate with him to town as the winds reached over forty miles per hour and the waves came lapping higher and higher toward the front door of the hotel. "Please, please come with me," he begged as he boarded the trolley with the rest of the guests headed for town. "No, she laughingly told him with a kiss, "I will stay here with the manager, he seems to think the hotel is safe, and I want to dance in the wind."

That is the last time he saw his beautiful young bride. The hotel was washed away in the storm, only a small south end section remained.

When hurricanes are approaching and waves are pounding Main Beach take a walk down there and mayhap you can find her dancing in the wind.

That Nassau Sound Affair

$\mathcal{W}$hat Captain Howlett says about it....A Solution Wanted: Captain A. A. Howlett came up to the city today. He was one of the four gentlemen who were at Mr. Roux house, by Nassau Sound last Saturday and Sunday night, where the strange and unnatural noises were heard by them. The young gentleman says he does not believe anymore in ghosts than anyone else, nor does either of the other three gentlemen who were with him, but there is a mystery about what was heard which he cannot solve, and which he would liberally contribute of his means to have cleared away. So far as being under the influence of strong drink is concerned, as some seem to think, he says that is without the least foundation whatever, and he is willing to sign an affidavit that not one drop of intoxicants was drank by Colonel Hart, General Ledwith, Captain Roberts or himself previous to hearing any of the noises.

They were all much fatigued, wet and anxious for sleep, and were awakened from a sound sleep by the strange noises. The moaning sounds, he thinks, were caused by the wind blowing down and through the crevices of the dirt chimney of the house. The bright coal-like spark of fire and the rapping of the chair legs on the floor is the mystery none can solve. At first they all thought it was someone trying to scare them from the outside of the old deserted house by means of a small wire or thread attached to the chair, but a diligent search and investigation failed to reveal any such agencies.

At one time a match was lighted in time to behold the chair standing on only two legs. The spark of fire was plainly seen by all while they were lying on the floor, but whenever they sat up and pursued it, it disappeared. Sunday night following these gentlemen remained at the house and kept a bright light burning and in devising a plan to keep the ghosts away, they agreed to sing and they all joined in that old familiar hymn, "Nearer My God to Thee," and made the woods echo with their melodious voices. Neither noise or sounds were heard that night after the men fell asleep.

What Captain Howlett wants, is some explanation of the strange occurrence. Can anyone give it?

- This story is from an old newspaper clipping (date unknown) and courtesy of The Amelia Island Museum of History.

Printed in the United States
151215LV00005B/1/P

9 781438 938189